My Mate Molly
and
My Chum Charlie

Written by C. Selbherr
Illustrated by M. Kahn

For my girls and our wonderful pets.

My mate Molly is short and sweet.

She has great **big** ears and tiny feet.

She follows me around wherever I go.

To the attic up high and the cellar down low.

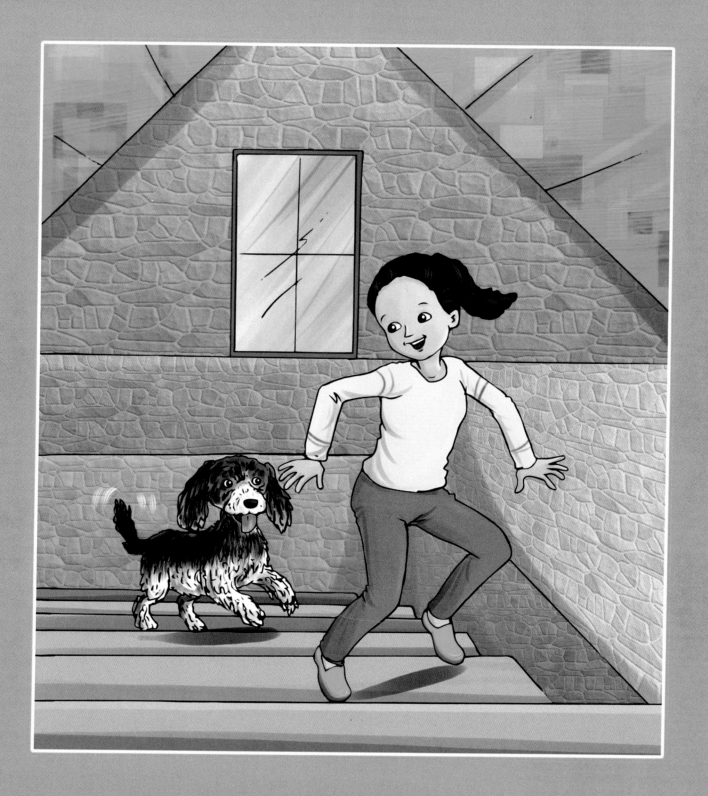

Her fur is curly and sometimes it grows,

Right down her legs and over her toes.

She wakes me at night when she wants to play,

But I'm so tired that I have to say:

"Go to sleep, little Molly, you silly thing.

No playing, no laughing, please do not sing!"

Her eyes are **large** and **big** and brown.

She's always kind; she deserves a crown.

She's **black**, she's white, she's fun and jolly.

She's furry and friendly, she's my mate Molly.

My chum Charlie is small and hairy,

With a long white beard but not at all scary.

He waits for me to come home from school.

Wagging his tail, he looks really cool.

He likes to walk and he loves to run,

Jumping in puddles and having fun.

He loves to bathe and have a wash,

Splashing in the water…

splish, splash, splosh!

He always barks when someone knocks at the door.

"Be quiet Charlie!
What are you growling for?"

He's there to protect us, the boss of the street,

Guarding and patrolling, quick on his feet.

He's such a good boy, he loves my mum.

He's the best, the greatest;
He's Charlie my chum!

Books by C. Selbherr

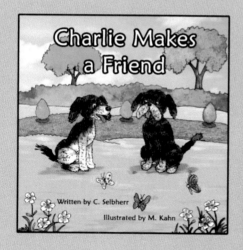

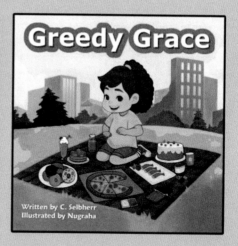

US and UK versions available
www.harlescottbooks.com

Made in the USA
Middletown, DE
30 July 2019